Philippa
P Phi

CW00853807

Little Grey Rabbit
and the Weasels

The Little Grey Rabbit Library

Little Grey Rabbit and the Weasels

Alison Uttley
pictures by Margaret Tempest

Collins

William Collins Sons & Co Ltd
London · Glasgow · Sydney · Auckland
Toronto · Johannesburg

First published 1947
© text The Alison Uttley Literary Property Trust 1986
© illustrations The Estate of Margaret Tempest 1986
© this arrangement William Collins Sons & Co Ltd 1986
Cover decoration by Fiona Owen
Decorated capital by Mary Cooper
Alison Uttley's original story has been abridged for this book.
Uttley, Alison
Little Grey Rabbit and the Weasels. —
Rev. ed. — (Little Grey Rabbit books)
I. Title   II. Tempest, Margaret
III. Series
823'.912 [J] PZ7

ISBN 0-00-194221-2

All rights reserved. No part of this
publication may be reproduced, stored
in a retrieval system, or transmitted,
in any form or by any means, electronic,
mechanical, photocopying, recording or
otherwise, without the prior permission
of William Collins Sons & Co Ltd,
8 Grafton Street, LONDON W1X 3LA.

Made and Printed in Great Britain by
William Collins Sons and Co Ltd, Glasgow

FOREWORD

Of course you must understand that Grey Rabbit's home had no electric light or gas, and even the candles were made from pith of rushes dipped in wax from the wild bees' nests, which Squirrel found. Water there was in plenty, but it did not come from a tap. It flowed from a spring outside, which rose up from the ground and went to a brook. Grey Rabbit cooked on a fire, but it was a wood fire, there was no coal in that part of the country. Tea did not come from India, but from a little herb known very well to country people, who once dried it and used it in their cottage homes. Bread was baked from wheat ears, ground fine, and Hare and Grey Rabbit gleaned in the cornfields to get the wheat.

The doormats were plaited rushes, like country-made mats, and cushions were stuffed with wool gathered from the hedges where sheep pushed through the thorns. As for the looking-glass, Grey Rabbit found the glass, dropped from a lady's handbag, and Mole made a frame for it. Usually the animals gazed at themselves in the still pools as so many country children have done. The country ways of Grey Rabbit were the country ways known to the author.

Down in the dell lived a family of Weasels. They had a dark little house, built against a wall where nobody could see it. There were two rooms upstairs and two rooms down and a scullery as well. The door was hidden behind a curtain of foxglove leaves, and the foxglove bells rang when anybody passed. The narrow windows were covered with green moss. Only in the middle of each there was a tiny crack where the Weasels peeped out at passers-by.

"There goes Milkman Hedgehog," they cried, as Old Hedgehog walked slowly past. Then one of them would leap downstairs, slip out of doors and run as softly as a shadow after him.

Sometimes a Weasel dipped a mug in the can of milk without Hedgehog knowing. Sometimes a Weasel tripped him up and drank the milk.

One day Speckledy Hen was strolling that way with a basket of eggs on her arm. She was taking them to little Grey Rabbit. It was a sunny day and she sang a nice little clucking song as she went along the narrow path. This is what she sang –

"Clucketty, Clucketty, Cluck.
My eggs will bring Good Luck.
Little Grey Rabbit, and Squirrel and Hare,
Will each have one and one to spare.
Clucketty, Clucketty, Cluck."

She passed close to the Weasels' house, but she did not know it was there.

"Three brown eggs and one to spare. How many is that?" asked Bad William Weasel.

"Five eggs," said Bad Winkie Weasel.

"No, it's four," said Bad Winnie Weasel.

"Be quick and get them," whispered William.

Out they slipped and away after the
Speckledy Hen. They stole the eggs from
under the white cloth, and the little Hen
walked on, knowing nothing.

"Clucketty, Clucketty, Cluck.
My eggs will bring Good Luck.
Two for Grey Rabbit, I declare,
One for Squirrel and one for Hare,
To make them a supper rich and rare.
Clucketty, Clucketty, Cluck."

She stepped daintily through the daisies,
up to Grey Rabbit's house. She tapped on the
door with her beak.
"Grey Rabbit, Grey Rabbit," she called.
Downstairs scuttered Grey Rabbit.
"Oh, my dear Speckledy Hen! How glad I
am to see you!" she cried.
"My dear Grey Rabbit! This is a pleasure!"
said the Speckledy Hen.

"Take a seat, dear Speckledy," said Grey Rabbit, drawing forward the rocking chair.

"Thank you, dear Grey Rabbit," said the Speckledy Hen. "I've never perched on a swinging chair before," said she, swaying to and fro. "It's remarkably soothing."

"Hare likes rocking, too," laughed Grey Rabbit. "Here he comes," she added, as Hare came bouncing in, followed by Squirrel.

"Hallo, Speckledy Hen!" cried Hare.

"Welcome," said Squirrel, shaking the Hen's wing.

"Have you brought something in that basket?" asked Hare.

Speckledy Hen smiled. "Do you like eggs, Hare?" she asked.

"I do!" replied Hare, licking his lips.

"Well, look in my basket! Lift the cover carefully, or they may bite you," said the Speckledy Hen.

Hare twitched the cloth from the basket.

"Oh! It's empty!" he cried.

The Speckledy Hen flew out of the chair and stared into the basket.

"I put in quite a lot of eggs," said she. "One for Hare and one for Squirrel and two for Grey Rabbit."

"Four eggs, all gone!" cried Grey Rabbit.

"Did you leave the basket anywhere?" asked Squirrel.

The Speckledy Hen shook her little head.

"A master-thief," said Hare.

"A magical trick," said Squirrel.

"A riddle of riddles," said Grey Rabbit.

They gave the Speckledy Hen a glass of wine and a cake, and they talked of eggs and eggs.

"I'll go home another way," said the Speckledy Hen.

Another day Moldy Warp was walking down the lane. He carried his little axe over his shoulder.

"I'll cut a nice pithy branch from an elder tree and make a whistle-pipe," said he. "Then I'll play a tune outside Grey Rabbit's window."

He went slowly past the Weasels' house, and he looked up at the fine foxglove growing there. He saw nothing of the fierce eyes watching his movements.

"Here's a big foxglove. I could cut it down if I wanted," he thought, and he leaned his axe against the foxglove stem. The foxglove bells tinkled, and the Weasels stared down at him.

He did not hear their whispers, nor see the skinny paw that snatched the axe away.

16

He fumbled in his pocket for his pipe, and as he searched for it he hummed a tune. This is what he hummed:

"Hum-mm-mm. It's a very nice day.
Hum-mm-mm. I'm going to play
Hum-mm-mm. On my whistle tonight,
Hum-mm-mm. For Grey Rabbit's delight."

He struck a light with his tinder-box and puffed at the lavender baccy.

Somebody snatched the pipe from his lips, and before he could turn round, another Weasel dragged his waistcoat over his head.

"Help! Help! Robbers! Thieves!" shouted Mole, muffled by a little hard fist. The waistcoat came off, and Mole was left staring about.

"Was it the wind?" he cried. "I heard nobody, I saw nobody, but something took my waistcoat. Who was it?"

He trotted quickly along the tiny green path to Grey Rabbit's house and told his story.

"Poor old Moldy Warp!" said Grey Rabbit, wrapping a rug round him. "I'll make you a new waistcoat tonight."

"Poor old Moldy Warp," said Hare. "I'll give you my axe."

"Poor old Moldy Warp!" said Squirrel. "I'll make you a briar pipe."

Mole sat in the rocking chair, shaking his head.

"It's very kind of you, my friends, but what I want to know is, how did my pipe and axe and waistcoat go? They vanished. They flew!"

"There's some mystery in the little lane," said Hare. "Let's call it Shady Lane."

"Stay here tonight, Moldy Warp," begged Grey Rabbit. "I'll put a shakedown bed in the kitchen for you."

Moldy Warp was delighted. He had never slept in the little house and he enjoyed the evening with his friends. Grey Rabbit cut out a little woollen waistcoat and stitched it with neat stitches in scarlet thread, and embroidered a few daisies down the front. Squirrel made a briar pipe and filled it with dried lavender. Hare sat and talked and told all his old tales.

When the moon came out Grey Rabbit put a couple of blankets on the floor and a little pillow stuffed with feathers for Moldy Warp.

Then they said goodnight, and Moldy Warp lay down on the hearthrug by Grey Rabbit's fire.

"Too-whit, Too-whoo," called Wise Owl, flying over the roof.

Mole raised himself for a moment to look at the nice new waistcoat Grey Rabbit had made. It hung on a chair near. Then he lay down and fell fast asleep. Although the bad Weasels were running and skipping about in the lanes and woods, the good fairies took care of all the little animals in Grey Rabbit's house.

The Weasels were enjoying themselves in their secret house. They crept out at night and got plenty to eat. During the day they robbed any one who went by. Cock Robin, the postman, lost his mail-bag. The Weasels didn't eat the letters, they tossed them away, but they found a few parcels wrapped in leaves, containing birthday presents of cakes and nuts.

"A queer thing. My letter-bag disappeared from my back," said the Robin. "I was tying my handkerchief in a knot to remember to be careful in Shady Lane, and lo! the bag was whisked away like magic."

Water-rat lost his frills one afternoon. Fuzzypeg lost his lesson-bag with all his homework.

Only Wise Owl and Grey Rabbit had not been troubled. Squirrel had the green bow nipped off her tail. Hare had his watch stolen, and his handkerchief taken from his pocket.

"I ran like the wind, or my coat would have gone from my back," he cried, when he got home. "You mustn't go down Shady Lane, Grey Rabbit. It isn't safe."

Grey Rabbit didn't want to go down Shady Lane. She thought she might lose her little blue apron. Then, one day, she was late coming home from market, and she took the short cut past the tall foxglove where the Weasels' house was hidden. Her little basket was filled with good things. There was barley-sugar for Hare, and a loaf of honey bread and some biscuits, and a piece of cloth to make Squirrel a dress.

Grey Rabbit hurried along the lane, holding her basket tight, looking here and there, keeping a watch for robbers. She was rather frightened, so she sang a little song.

"The sun and the moon came down
one day,
To live in the animals' wood.
They kept them safe, and drove away
The wicked and helped the good."

The Weasels were watching her from their mossy windows.

"Hush! Hush!" they whispered. "We'll catch her, basket and all."

They crept down to the door and looked outside. The little Rabbit was singing as she came past. Then the foxglove bells began to ring, and the Weasels went on tiptoes in the shadows.

Suddenly William Weasel snatched her basket, and Winkie and Winnie leapt from the leaves and picked her up.

"Oh dear me! Oh dear!" cried Grey Rabbit. "Please let me go home."

"No, Grey Rabbit! We've been waiting for you," said the Weasels, chuckling. "We are not going to eat *you*. Oh, no! We want somebody to bake and wash and clean. We want somebody to make our beds."

"Please, I have to go home to look after Squirrel and Hare," said Grey Rabbit. "They can't do without me."

"They must. Here you are, and here you will stay. Nobody will find you."

So Grey Rabbit knew she must make the best of it. She cooked for the fierce Weasels, and cleaned their ugly little house.

She polished the rusty tins and saucepans, she scrubbed the floor, and washed the clothes. She worked all day without stopping, or they nipped her with their sharp teeth.

At night she slept in one of the little bedrooms, and in the next room was Winnie, the worst of them all. Grey Rabbit lay down on the rough bed, and wrapped her apron around her. The stars shone through the tiny crack in the window, and the wind blew under the door. Downstairs the Weasels were laughing and clinking their glasses. They were rejoicing they had caught Grey Rabbit.

In Grey Rabbit's house there was great trouble. Hare and Squirrel searched everywhere for their friend. Hare even ventured to Wise Owl's tree and rang the bell.

"Grey Rabbit gone?" hooted Wise Owl. "Very careless of you, Hare. Go home and find her."

Poor Hare turned sadly away, and Wise Owl called him back.

"I'll help you, Hare. You look by day and I'll hunt by night."

Hare ventured down Shady Lane, looking for Grey Rabbit's basket. He passed the Weasels' house, but there was no sound, or sight of any one.

Then out darted a Weasel and grabbed Hare's clean pocket handkerchief, which he had taken to wave as a truce to Wise Owl. Hare scurried home in a fright.

Grey Rabbit saw the handkerchief, with the letter H in the corner. "Poor old Hare," she thought, sadly. "His Sunday hanky."

That night, the Weasels fetched her from work in the scullery to the kitchen where they sat round the fire.

"Sing to us, Grey Rabbit," they commanded.

"I'll sing if you promise not to hurt my friends, or take their things," said Grey Rabbit. "I won't sing a note unless you promise."

She stood there like a little grey rock, and she wouldn't open her mouth.

"We promise," said the Weasels at last.

So Grey Rabbit straightened her apron, and raised her head and sang to the Weasels.

Grey Rabbit sang many a song: "Mowing the Barley" and "Strawberry Fair" and "There was a Jolly Miller."

How the Weasels clapped and stamped and shouted "Hurrah".

Wise Owl was flying slowly down Shady Lane, listening to the rustle of leaves and flowers.

"What's that noise?" he asked himself.

He flew down on his silent wings and waited there. He could hear the stamping and squeaking. Then he heard a well-known little voice singing "Rule Britannia." He flew close and put one eye to the mossy window. He could just see inside the room. A candle was burning on the table, the Weasels sat round and Grey Rabbit was singing.

"Too-whit, Too-whoo," called Wise Owl loudly, and the candle was blown out and the Weasels were quiet.

"Hush! Go to bed, Grey Rabbit. There's that pesky Owl flying over. Go to bed," said they. "He'll eat you up if he sees you."

So Grey Rabbit went up the crooked stair to her room. She pressed her face to the window crack, and Wise Owl saw her.

"Oh, Wise Owl! Save me!" she whispered, and she opened the window. Wise Owl broke away the moss, and balanced on the sill.

Grey Rabbit climbed on his back and clung to his feathers. Away he flew, but the tip of his wing caught the foxglove and set all the bells ringing.

"What's that? The bells ringing an alarm!" cried the Weasels. They were too late. Wise Owl and Grey Rabbit had gone.

Wise Owl dropped her gently on her own doorstep, and then he flew off.

"Hare! Squirrel! Here I am! Let me in!" called Grey Rabbit, banging at the door.

Hare and Squirrel came tumbling downstairs, half-asleep.

"Grey Rabbit! Where have you been? How did you get home?" they asked, as they brought her in and locked the door again.

"Wise Owl saved me!" said Grey Rabbit. "He did! He did! I flew on his back."

"On the Owl's back?" echoed Hare and Squirrel, astonished.

Now Wise Owl had flown away to the Weasels' house.

"Ho, all you Weasel tribe!" said he. "Pack up your belongings and depart at once. If you are here tomorrow I shall make a meal of you. Take warning, and you must leave behind everything you stole."

That was all, but the Weasels knew he meant it. They packed their little hand-cart with their pots and pans and chairs and bedding, and put the table on the top.

"Don't forget Mole's waistcoat," they said, "and Hare's handkerchiefs, and the watch, and the axe, and the schoolbag. There's an empty house far away where we can settle before any one is awake."

Then Wise Owl flew over just as they were starting.

"Have you left the stolen goods?" he asked sternly.

So the Weasels had to take off all the treasures they had thieved.

The next day Grey Rabbit set off with a basket of presents for Wise Owl. She rang the little bell at his doorway and waved her handkerchief.

"Who's that, waking me up?" yawned Wise Owl. "Oh, it's you, Grey Rabbit. I'm glad you are none the worse for your flight."

"It was lovely, Wise Owl," cried Grey Rabbit. "I've brought you an apple pasty and a treacle tart, and a bottle of primrose wine."

Down to the ground flew Wise Owl, and fluttered his wide wings.

"Just sing that song again, Grey Rabbit, the song you were singing to the Weasels," said he.

So Grey Rabbit sang:

"Rule Britannia,
Britannia rules the waves,
Britons Never, Never, Never, shall be
Slaves!"

"Ah! She's an old friend of mine, that Britannia," said Wise Owl.